W9-AZQ-047

Librarian Reviewer

Joanne Bongaarts
Educational Consultant
MS in Library Media Education, Minnesota State University, Mankato
Teacher and Media Specialist with Edina Public Schools, MN, 1993–2000

Reading Consultant

Elizabeth Stedem
Educator/Consultant, Colorado Springs, CO
MA in Elementary Education, University of Denver, CO

First published in the United States in 2007
by Stone Arch Books,
151 Good Counsel Drive, P.O. Box 669,
Mankato, Minnesota 56002.
www.stonearchbooks.com

First published by Evans Brothers Ltd,
2A Portman Mansions, Chiltern Street,
London W1U 6NR, United Kingdom.

Copyright © 2004 Robin and Chris Lawrie

This edition published under license from Evans Brothers Ltd.
All rights reserved. No part of this publication may be reproduced
in whole or in part, or stored in a retrieval system, or transmitted in any
form or by any means, electronic, mechanical, photocopying, recording,
or otherwise, without written permission of the publisher.

Library of Congress Cataloging-in-Publication Data
Lawrie, Robin.
    Paintball Panic / by Robin and Chris Lawrie; illustrated by Robin
Lawrie.
        p. cm. — (Ridge Riders)
    Summary: Slam Duncan and his fellow mountain bikers refuse to
let property developers take over the hill where they train, but when the
developers try to gain support with a paintball weekend, their fun quickly
backfires.
    ISBN-13: 978-1-59889-126-3 (library binding)
    ISBN-10: 1-59889-126-X (library binding)
    ISBN-13: 978-1-59889-274-1 (paperback)
    ISBN-10: 1-59889-274-6 (paperback)
    [1. All terrain cycling—Fiction. 2. Paintball (Game)—Fiction.]
I. Lawrie, Christine. II. Title. III. Series: Lawrie, Robin. Ridge Riders.
PZ7.L438218Pa 2007
[Fic]—dc22   2006005964

1 2 3 4 5 6 11 10 09 08 07 06

Printed in the United States of America

PAINTBALL PANIC

by Robin and Chris Lawrie
illustrated by Robin Lawrie

STONE ARCH BOOKS
MINNEAPOLIS   SAN DIEGO

The Ridge Riders

 Hi, my name is "Slam" Duncan.

This is Aziz. We call him Dozy.

Then there's Larry.

This is Fiona.

And Andy.

I'm Andy. (Andy is deaf. He uses sign language instead of talking.)

I ride and race downhill mountain bikes with a group of my friends. We call ourselves "The Ridge Riders."

We train on a big hill called Westridge behind our town, Shabberley.

Sometimes there are races there, too. For a long time everything was just great. But recently there have been problems.

I'm Larry.

I'm Aziz.

Call me "Dozy."

I'm Fiona.

Lots of new people have moved into our town. They all want to use our hill, too. But not for mountain biking.

Woof woof woof YAP YAP YAP!

Dog walkers use our trails!

So do joggers.

Some days we just have to give up and go home, but even that can be difficult.

Suddenly our quiet little lanes are full of traffic! It's horrible!

8

I talked to my dad about it.

The next day the Riders met at the Westridge parking lot.

That night I had a great idea.
I'd make a petition for all
the new people who use
the hill. I'd tell them
what was happening.
I'd get lots of signatures.
First I tried the dog walkers.

Yes!

Not my problem. I can walk the dog anywhere. And my daughter needs a house in town.

GRRR!!!

Then the joggers.

No way. I'm a builder, and I could use some work. I can jog anywhere.

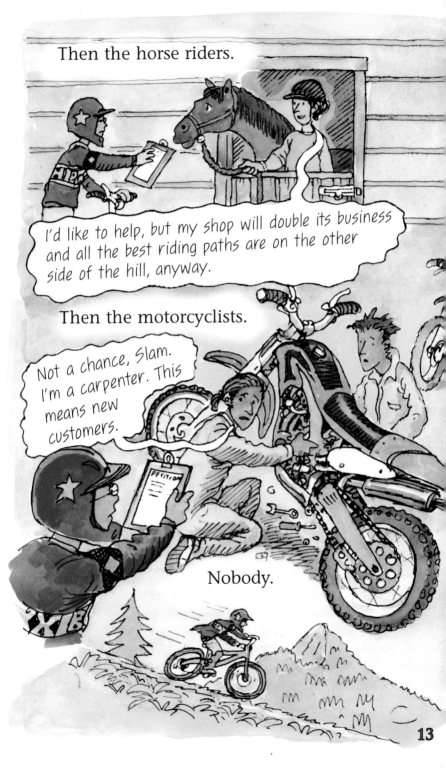

On the way home from school, we looked in the Tuer Cycles store window.

It was a surprise!

Later, on my paper route, I was talking to
Miss Soames, the sheep farmer.

On the way home I caught up with Fiona on the edge of Westridge. She was having problems with her horse. Horses can be startled by bikes coming up quietly behind them. I should have let her know I was coming!

Well, Slam, that's just typical of your behavior. Dozy and I are pretty fed up with the whole paintball business. We all know where playing with guns ends up.

I could see her point. But Larry, Andy, and I had decided to give paintball a try. We couldn't back out now. Besides, it looked like fun.

Saturday was the day of the Westridge Development's paintball tournament. The paintballers caused a huge traffic jam and managed to upset just about everyone, including . . .

Miss Soames and her dog, a horse rider, a couple of hikers, and Fiona's dad on his tractor. A paintballer splatted a motorcyclist's leather jacket with a paintball. Good thing the owner didn't see who did it!

At the Westridge parking lot, the organizers explained paintball rules.

Welcome to Westridge Development's
PAINTBALLING!

Good morning. The rules of this game are simple. If you get splatted with any color paintball on the head or torso, you're out. No arguments. Enjoy!

Sounds good to me!

Punk's dad is renting stuff. It's probably not great, but that's okay.

Punk Tuer, our biking rival, appeared with a shiny new gun.

The game began. Everybody was splatting everybody. Andy, Larry, and I laid low.

Then everybody argued about who was out or not.

So it was game over for the Ridge Riders.
On the way back to the gun rental . . .

25

I went straight home, but Andy and Larry went the long way over the hills. That evening Andy texted me what happened.

Fiona had come roaring up to them.

27

But as I was reading
the text message . . .

. . . lots of angry people were gathering
outside. Dog walkers, joggers, horse riders,
and farmers.

Come outside, Slam. We want to talk to you!

I knew there was no point in hiding.
So I went to the door.

Okay, Slam, where's that petition? We don't want this paintballing nonsense every weekend. WESTRIDGE DEVELOPMENT **MUST GO!**

About the Author and Illustrator

Robin and Chris Lawrie wrote the *Ridge Riders* books together, and Robin illustrated them. Their inspiration for these books is their son. They wanted to write books that he would find interesting. Many of the *Ridge Riders* books are based on adventures he and his friends had while biking. Robin and Chris live in England, and will soon be moving to a big, old house that is also home to sixty bats.

Glossary

branding (BRAN-ding)—marking, identifying

deaf (DEF)—not being able to hear well or to hear at all

economic (ek-uh-NOM-ik)—anything related to business or money

panic (PAN-ik)—a sudden feeling of great fear

petition (puh-TISH-uhn)—a special request, usually in writing, to someone in charge

shear (SHEER)—to remove the wool or hair from an animal with scissors or shears

sign (SINE)—to use sign language (a method of communication that uses hand movements)

texted (TEXT-IHD)—sent a message (on a cell phone)

Internet Sites

Do you want to know more about subjects related to this book? Or are you interested in learning about other topics? Then check out FactHound, a fun, easy way to find Internet sites.

Our investigative staff has already sniffed out great sites for you!

Here's how to use FactHound:

1. Visit *www.facthound.com*

2. Select your grade level.

3. To learn more about subjects related to this book, type in the book's ISBN number: **159889126X**.

4. Click the **Fetch It** button.

FactHound will fetch the best Internet sites for you!

Discussion Questions

1. How do you feel about towns and cities changing and growing bigger? What is good about it? What is not good about it? Discuss the pros and cons of development. (Think about how some of the characters feel in this story.)

2. On page 9, Slam says that their town isn't worth living in anymore. Why does he think that? Read his father's response. How does his dad feel?

3. Were you surprised that the boys paintballed the sheep? Why or why not?

Writing Prompts

1. Andy and Larry got into trouble when they paintballed the sheep. Have you ever played a game or sport when things went too far? Did someone get hurt or something get damaged? Write about it.

2. Slam tries to get people to sign his petition. He wants them all to complain about the big company changing the hill and ruining their bike paths. Do you have a special place where you like to play or hang out with your friends? What would you do if someone decided to change it without asking you? Would you write a petition or do something else? Write and tell us.

Read other adventures of the Ridge Riders

Cheat Challenge

Slam Duncan and his friends, the Ridge Riders, don't know what to think when they come across a sword buried deep in their mountain-biking course. It's part of a new racing course contest called Excalibur. Then Slam accidentally gets a look at the map of the course, but he knows he can't tell his teammates the map's secrets.

Fear 3.1

While rock climbing, Slam loses his foothold. Luckily, his safety harness holds, but that doesn't stop Slam from being terrified. Soon, he can't even manage to complete the mountain biking courses he's ridden on for years. Will Slam ever get over his fear?

Snow Bored

The Ridge Riders are bored. So much snow has fallen on their mountain biking practice hill that they can't ride. Luckily, Dozy has a great idea. He turns an old skateboard and a pair of sneakers into a snowboard. Before long, everyone is snowboarding.

White Lightning

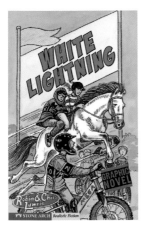

Someone smashed the Ridge Riders' practice jumps, and they suspect Fiona and her horse-riding friends. The boys are so mean to Fiona that she leaves. Then Slam gets a flat tire and has to race back home to get his spare, and he only has 50 minutes! Now a horse would come in handy!

Check out Stone Arch Books graphic novels!

Sam's Goal
Michael Hardcastle

When England's top goal-scorer invites Sam to his next soccer game, he can't believe it. The problem is, neither do Sam's friends.

My Brother's a Keeper
Michael Hardcastle

It looks like the Raiders are out of luck when their goalie is injured right before the big game. Luckily, Carlo has a new stepbrother who just happens to play goal.